6 Six-Minute Bedtime Stories

For lovers of Tea Parties, Mermaids, Pirates, Fairies, Space Racers and Witches.

By Doug Parker

This book is dedicated to my darling wife, Paulene.

My deepest thanks to my father for being such an inspiration for me.

Many special thanks to Suzanne J.; Dominic and Iroha H.; Cheryl, Gilad and Harrie H.; Kimberley, John, Gianna and Julianna P.

Front cover design by: Lisa Fox

About the Author

Husband. Father. Groomer. Author.

With his days dedicated to his family, "Uncle Doug" (as he is known to his doggy friends) has taken to working as an author by night. A lover of reading from an early age, he has spent many years practicing his craft and now hopes to pass on that love to the next generation.

To find other works by this author, visit: www.dougparkerauthor.com

ISBN: 978-0-947481-91-9
First Published: August 2020

Contents

Messy Margaret's Magical Tea Party

When Margaret awoke she looked outside. The morning sun was shining among puffy white clouds, the green grass looked soft and inviting, and birds sang sweetly to welcome new flowers.

"What a perfect day for a garden party," she said.

Getting out of bed she clambered over piles of clothes, tottered between towers of toys and shuffled between stacks of books. Following the smell of toast and eggs she found her mother in the kitchen making breakfast.

"Mom," Margaret said as she buttered a piece of toast. "May I invite Kim and Shawna for a garden party this afternoon?"

"I think that might be okay," said her mother. "But I'm quite busy so you'll have to do the preparations yourself."

"What?" said Margaret. "Even the tea and sandwiches?"

"I'll make the sandwiches," said her mother. "But you have to make the tea, I showed you how yesterday. And you must tidy up your room, I'm sure your guests wouldn't want to have tea surrounded by piles of clothes."

"It's going to be a garden tea party mommy," said Margaret. "We'll be outside all afternoon, so there's no need to clean up my room."

Her mother crossed her arms. "You will clean your room or there will be no party. Margaret, you can't even see the floor in there!"

After breakfast Margaret started to pick up her clothes to put them in the laundry basket, when she found her invitation to Kim's birthday party.

"Of course!" Margaret said. "I must have proper cards to invite them. Mom! Where are my art supplies? I have to make invitations for Kim and Shawna!"

"Your art supplies are in your room," said her mother. "If your clothes were put away you might find them quite easily."

Margaret sighed and went back to putting her clothes in the laundry basket. She even started to put her books on their shelves when she finally found her art supplies. Sitting down at her desk, she soon finished two cards inviting her friends to come for tea.

Stepping over the toys still scattered on her bedroom floor, Margaret went to the kitchen where her mother was now making lunch.

"I've made my invitations for Kim and Shawna," said Margaret, showing them to her mother.

"Oh Margaret, these are lovely!" said her mother. "Well done."

"Thank you," said Margaret. "Kim and Shawna don't live far. May I deliver their invitations after lunch?"

"Only if you've finished tidying your room," said her mother. "And you'd better hurry, I see dark clouds outside. I think it's going to rain soon."

"It can't," said Margaret. "Not today!"

Margaret ate her lunch quickly and then raced to put her toys away. With her mother's approval, she skipped down the street to her friends' houses. Both Kim and Shawna thanked Margaret for their lovely invitations and promised to come for tea.

As Margaret headed home a drop of rain splattered on the ground.

"Oh no," she said. Margaret began running up the street as fast as she could. She barely made it home before the rain bucketed down!

"Mommy, whatever shall I do?" wailed Margaret. "Kim and Shawna both said they were coming to my garden party but now it's pouring!"

Her mother gave her a hug. "I'm so sorry," she said. "I know how much you wanted your friends to come and play. Should we telephone to have them come another day?"

Margaret shook her head. "Kim's party is in two days and she will be busy tomorrow." She sighed. "I suppose we will have to have the tea party in my room, like you said."

Her mother smiled. "I'm sure it will be the best garden party ever," she said.

"It won't be a garden party if it's in my room, mommy" said Margaret.

"Maybe we can fix that," said her mother, and gave her a wink.

So Margaret got out her art supplies and drew pictures of flowers, trees and fairies, which she hung up around her room. Her mother went into her sewing cupboard and found green fabric and strings of festival lights, which she draped around Margaret's bedroom.

"There," said her mother as she turned on the festival lights. "Now it looks like you're in a real garden."

Margaret clapped. "My room looks like a magic garden! Oh thank you mommy!" She hugged her mother tightly. "I'm sorry I made such a fuss earlier. If I hadn't cleaned up my room we wouldn't have been able to make it magical."

Just then there was a knock on the front door. When Margaret opened it, she found Kim and Shawna huddled under their umbrellas.

"Come in, come in," said Margaret. "And come to my magic garden tea party… in my room!"

When they saw how lovely Margaret's room was, Kim and Shawna both agreed it was absolutely perfect. While Margaret helped her mother to make the tea and sandwiches, Shawna and Kim drew more pictures and hung them up. Then the three friends ate, drank tea and played together for a very long time, until Kim and Shawna had to go home.

When Margaret got into bed that night she was very tired after such a busy day.

"Good night mommy," she said between yawns. "I'm sorry my room is a mess again. I promise to clean it up in the morning."

"That's okay my dear," said her mother, tucking her into her bed. "This may be messy for a bedroom, but it's perfect for a magic garden."

After kisses and hugs, Margaret rolled over and was soon fast asleep.

The Mermaid and the Wampus

Melody Mermaid was on a mission. She had been practicing her special song in the quiet of the kelp forest for the Grand Mermaid Concert, when her voice vanished.

Her mother told her that her voice must have been stolen by a slimy wampus, a half-walrus half-octopus creature who lurked in the kelp forest. They were masters of disguise, hiding among kelp leaves or making themselves look like rocks. You could swim right past one and never know, but there was a way to find them. Slimy wampuses were always humming if they thought they were alone.

So Melody hid in the kelp forest, straining her ears to hear the hum of a slimy wampus. A school of fish swam past, inviting her to play. She tried to say 'no thanks', but without her voice nothing came out.

"What's the matter?" said something in the kelp leaves. "Wampus got your tongue?"

Melody leapt up and looked in all directions. She saw nothing but kelp. "Where are you?" she yelled, or tried to yell, but nothing came out.

"Oh dear," said the voice. "A wampus *has* got your

tongue." Some of the kelp leaves uncurled and changed into what could only be a slimy wampus.

Melody glared at the wampus and jabbed her finger at her mouth.

"I'm sorry your voice was taken," the wampus said. "But don't get mad at me. I didn't do it."

Melody crossed her arms and stared.

"Don't you know anything?" asked the wampus. "If I stole your voice you would have it back by now, because as soon as I opened my mouth it would escape."

Melody's spirits fell. She had found a wampus, but not the right one!

"My name is Henry," said the wampus. "There aren't many of us around here. Let's go see my sister, she's close by."

Henry led the way through the kelp forest. He swam very slowly, humming as he went. Melody kept swimming too fast and almost lost Henry several times. She only found him again because of his constant humming. Forced to swim more slowly, she found Henry's humming rather pleasant, and he didn't really look slimy at all now that he wasn't pretending to be a piece of kelp.

Eventually, Henry stopped. He reached out and gently tapped a rock. "Hey Sarah, open up," he said. "It's okay, she's a friend."

The rock opened two very worried looking eyes, before uncurling into a very little wampus.

"Come on," said Henry. "Say hello."

Sarah shook her head and said nothing.

"Sarah, have you seen this mermaid before?" asked

Henry.

Silence.

Henry looked at Melody. "I'm so sorry. She's only little and doesn't understand." Henry turned back to Sarah. "Are you hungry?" he asked.

Sarah nodded.

"Would you like your special treat?" asked Henry.

Sarah nodded again and gave a shy smile.

"Sarah really likes the kelp leaves that grow right at the surface," said Henry. "I'll go get some and when she opens her mouth to eat your voice will escape. Then everything will be back to normal."

Melody shook her head. It was kind of Henry to offer to go, but the time for the concert was fast approaching and he swam so slowly! She pointed to herself and then up to the surface.

"You will be much faster," Henry said. "But how will you find us again? The kelp is very thick here."

Melody smiled, pointed at Henry, and then cupped her hand to her ear.

"Of course!" said Henry. "I'll hum as loudly as I can. You'll be sure to find us then!"

Melody rushed to the surface. It was getting hard to see as the sun was almost down. She picked as many of the kelp leaves as she could manage, then dove back down to the bottom. Melody listened intently. There! She swam quickly towards the sound of Henry's humming.

"Hooray!" shouted Henry as Melody burst through the kelp leaves.

It took a moment, but Sarah finally grabbed the kelp and began to eat. Melody felt all tingly!

"Did it work?" she tried to say. No, she did say! "Yipee! It worked!" Melody gave Henry a big hug. "Thank you so much Henry, for all your help."

"I'm so sorry," said Sarah. "I didn't mean to take your voice. I didn't even know I could do that yet!"

"I forgive you," said Melody. "Do you promise not to do it again?"

"I promise," said Sarah.

The kelp forest was getting darker. "I'm Melody," she said. "I'm sorry to have to go, but the Grand Mermaid Concert starts soon and I have to get back."

"Oh, I love that concert," said Henry. "Though I've never heard it up close. The mermaids normally chase me away in case I steal their voices." Henry huffed. "I've never done that to a mermaid and I never will."

"Well you can come tonight," said Melody. "As my guests."

"Oh can we?" asked Sarah. "Please Henry?"

Henry shook his head. "I'd like to more than anything, but we swim so slowly it will be over by the time we get there."

"You wampuses may be slow swimmers, but I'm quite fast," said Melody. She held out her hands. "Hold onto me and I'll get us all there in time!"

So off they went, Melody swimming as fast as she could and Henry helping her with directions through the kelp forest. It did take a long time but they made it to the mermaid village before the concert started. Melody explained everything to her mother and the other mermaids, who thanked Henry for being so helpful and apologized for chasing him away in the past.

The concert started and Melody sang with the other mermaids. Their singing was so beautiful that the song came to life and the water glowed as bright as the sun!

By the time the evening's celebrations finished, it was very late. Melody's mother invited Henry and Sarah to spend the night rather than swim home in the dark.

Worn out after such a long and exciting day, Melody said goodnight to her two new friends and soon fell fast asleep.

The Treasure of Captain Greenbeard

Molly stamped her foot in the sun-dried sand. "A treasure map Captain? A real one?"

"Yes Molly," said Emily. "It's real alright, and it will lead us to the lost treasure of Captain Greenbeard!"

"Squawk!" said Squawk the parrot.

Molly nodded. "The legends do say that Greenbeard hid a fabulous treasure before he was caught and sent to Davey-Jones."

"Do they say why he was called Greenbeard?" asked Emily.

"Not really Captain. Some say it was because he ate so much green pea soup his beard turned green," said Molly.

"Squawk!" said Squawk.

Molly shrugged. "Others say that he loved trees so much he grew them in his beard to keep them close while at sea."

"Both sound rather silly to me," said Emily as she looked at the map and then at the land around them. "The map shows a jungle trail between those hills. Let's go!"

So Emily, Molly and Squawk set off, following the

map's clues until they came to a clearing.

"This is the place," said Emily. "This clearing is where the X marks the spot."

"Hey-ho," said Molly. "What's this?"

It was a garden bed, well tended and ready for planting.

"That's odd," said Emily. "There's nobody on the island but us. Who's keeping the garden free of weeds?"

"I AM!" boomed a voice right behind them.

Emily and Molly jumped and turned around. It was the ghostly form of Captain Greenbeard!

"Booga-booga-booga!" shouted Greenbeard.

"Squawk!" screeched Squawk as he flew away.

"Eeek!" shrieked Emily and Molly as they turned and ran.

"Stop!" shouted Greenbeard. "Please no! Stop!"

Emily and Molly stopped, looked at each other, and then looked back at the ghost.

"Oh thank goodness," said Greenbeard. "You almost ran through my garden!"

"Sorry," said Emily. "But you gave us quite a fright."

Greenbeard shrugged. "Well of course. That's what ghosts do."

Molly scoffed. "Then why did you want us to stop? You're not going to scare us again."

"Do you know how hard it is to keep that garden free of weeds and the rows all neat just by shouting at them?" Greenbeard shook his head. "It's no joke without proper hands, let me tell you."

"Captain Greenbeard," said Emily. "We've come to claim your treasure." She waved the treasure map. "It's supposed to be here, so where is it?"

Greenbeard scowled. "That map was meant to go to a real pirate. Are you real pirates?"

"Well," said Emily. "We're here to plunder your plunder. Isn't that what a real pirate would do?"

"Perhaps," said Greenbeard.

"And we have a parrot," said Molly. "Though he's flown off now because you scared him."

"Squawk," said Squawk from a distant tree.

"A good point," said Greenbeard. "But real pirates are also good at figuring out clues on treasure maps."

Emily smiled. "We followed your clues here, didn't we?"

"Aye," said Greenbeard. "But that map was easy to follow. So I will give you a final test." He pointed to the jungle. "Over there is a shack with clues about what to do to get my treasure."

After Molly coaxed Squawk back to her shoulder, they all went to the old shack. Inside was a table. On it was an empty soup bowl, a spoon, a bucket full of dried up pea pods, and a jug of water that sparkled and shone.

"Looks like those legends are about to come in handy," whispered Emily to Molly.

"Aye," said Molly. "Here, why's this water all sparkly?"

"That's magic water," said Greenbeard. "I stole it from a water fairy. It will bring any plant back to life." He frowned. "I hear a weed sneaking into my garden. Come to me when you've figured out what to do." Shouting loudly, Greenbeard flew off.

"Hmm," said Emily. "Let's look around to see if there is anything else in this shack."

They searched. Molly found nothing. Emily found an old cook pot.

"Squawk!" said Squawk, who had found a piece of paper in the rafters.

"Great job Squawk," said Molly. She looked at the paper than gave it to Emily. "What's it say? Looks like a code!"

Emily smiled. "It is a code, or rather, a recipe for green pea soup!"

"The legend is true then," said Molly. "Do we have everything we need?"

"Yes," said Emily. "We just need a fire to boil the water. There was an old fire pit outside, we can use that."

So Squawk and Molly collected sticks for the fire while Emily put the dried up pea pods in the cooking pot. Greenbeard was still shouting in his garden.

"That's enough sticks," said Molly. "I'll get this fire going and we'll have pea soup and Greenbeard's treasure!"

"Wait," said Emily. "Something's not right. This is too easy, just like the map."

Molly frowned. "Well, what else can we do with what we have?"

"I'm not sure," said Emily. "It's hard to think with Greenbeard shouting so much."

Molly nodded. "He wasn't lying. It does take a lot of shouting to keep that garden bed clear."

Emily jumped up. "That's it! Bring the magic water Molly, and Squawk you bring the sticks."

The pirates returned to Greenbeard's garden.

"We know what to do Captain," said Emily.

"Do ya now?" growled Greenbeard. "Show me."

Emily walked carefully down the garden rows, using the spoon to make a small hole in the dirt after every step. Into each hole she placed a single dried up pea pod. Squawk came next, firmly planting a stick in the dirt next to each hole. Last came Molly, carefully pouring a few drops of the magic water on each pea pod before covering it with dirt. By the time they finished, the first shoots of new vines had poked out of the dirt, climbed the sticks and sprouted huge new pea pods.

"You did it!" shouted Greenbeard. "You solved my riddle. You are real pirates and deserve my treasure!"

Just then the huge pea pods split open and out tumbled giant peas made of solid gold!

"Hooray!" shouted Emily and Molly.

"Squawk!" screeched Squawk.

Greenbeard smiled. "Now I can go to my rest. Enjoy your treasure!" And with that, the ghostly captain disappeared.

Emily, Molly and Squawk spent the rest of the day harvesting the gold peas. They returned to their ship triumphant and very tired. Lying in their hammocks, they stared at their treasure until their eyes began to close.

"Good night Captain," said Molly.

"Good night Molly, and sweet dreams," said Emily.

"Squawk!"

And they all slept, happily ever after.

Fairy Cakes for the Queen

Little fairy Honeywheat was enjoying her morning tea when a squirrel bounded up to her.

"Excuse me miss," said the squirrel. "Is your name Honeywheat? The best baker of fairy cakes in the forest?"

Honeywheat laughed. "That's my name, and everyone always loves my fairy cakes so I guess so."

"Great! The Queen of Fairies," the squirrel paused and scratched his head. "Ah yes! The Queen requires your fairy cakes for her afternoon tea today."

"The Queen? What an honor," said Honeywheat. "Of course I will make some for her. How many does she need?"

The squirrel stopped playing with his tail. "Oh. I'm not sure. Lots I expect. I think she's having a party." With that, the squirrel bounded off.

"Well," said Honeywheat. "I better get cooking if I'm going to be ready by tea time!"

Soon, the whole forest around her home was filled with the delicious smell of freshly-baked fairy cakes. Honeywheat carefully packed a jar of honey into her carry-bag, which was so full and heavy with fairy cakes she couldn't fly!

"That's okay," she said to herself. "It's a lovely day for a walk and I've plenty of time." So off she went, singing her favorite song.

She had only been walking for a few minutes when she heard an "Ow!" in a familiar voice. Investigating she found Cuddles the hedgehog limping along.

"Whatever's the matter Cuddles?" asked Honeywheat.

Cuddles sat down. "Oh thank goodness," he wheezed. "I've been coming to see you all morning. I cut my paw last night trying to get my dinner and I haven't been able to walk properly since!"

Honeywheat examined the sore paw. "It does look tender." She opened her carry-pack and took out the jar of honey. She gently cleaned the cut, put a spot of honey on it and wrapped it in a spare napkin. "You'll need to keep it clean but it should be right as rain by tomorrow," she said.

Just then Cuddles' tummy rumbled so loudly Honeywheat looked around to see if there was a bear!

"Sorry," said Cuddles. "I didn't get much dinner last night and no breakfast this morning."

"That's okay," said Honeywheat with a laugh. "Here, have a few fairy cakes. I was so excited to be asked to make some for the Queen's tea party I made far too many!"

Now hedgehogs aren't very big, but Cuddles was very, very hungry. By the time he was full Honeywheat was getting worried about how many fairy cakes would be left!

Cuddles rubbed his tummy. "Those are delicious!

I'm sorry I ate so many."

"I'm glad you liked them," said Honeywheat as she shouldered her carry-pack. "Don't worry, there are lots left and my pack is light enough for me to fly now." After promising to check on him later, Honeywheat flew off. "Now that I'm flying I'll be at the Queen's palace in no time!" she said to herself, and started singing her favorite song again.

Barely a minute later, she heard baby sparrows squabbling loudly.

"What's all this noise about?" shouted Honeywheat as she flew up to the nest. Four sparrow chicks were shouting at each other and then at her. "Calm down, calm down," she said and pointed at one of the chicks. "You, what's your name?"

"I'm Featherweight," he said. "Because I'm the smallest!"

"Well then Featherweight, what's the matter?" asked Honeywheat.

"We're so hungry!" said Featherweight. "Petal-Beak found a bug but wouldn't share and-"

"I did not!" said Petal-Beak. "It was just a bit of a leaf!"

"Enough! Calm everyone!" said Honeywheat. "Where's your mother?"

"She left at dawn like normal—" said Petal-Beak.

"But she hasn't come back—" said Featherweight.

"We're so hungry!" chorused the sparrow chicks.

Honeywheat smiled. "Well, I can give you a snack to tide you over if you promise to stop fighting." She opened her carry-pack. The chicks' eyes went wide.

"Fairy cakes!" shrieked Petal-Beak. The four chicks

dove at Honeywheat's pack, snapping up fairy cakes in a blur of beaks. In a flash her pack was empty!

"Hey!" said Honeywheat. "That wasn't nice. Those were for the Queen's tea!"

"We're sorry," chirped the chicks, who didn't look sorry at all.

Just then, mother sparrow returned to the nest. "Here we are," she said. "Fat caterpillars for everyone! Oh, hello miss fairy. My chicks weren't causing a fuss were they?"

Honeywheat's lip trembled as she picked up her empty pack. "I think everything will be fine now," she said. She flew off, the chicks squabbling about which caterpillar was the biggest just as loudly as before.

She flew the rest of the way to the Queen's palace in silence. When she arrived, the Queen welcomed her. "Oh Honeywheat, I'm so glad you could make it—"

Honeywheat burst into tears. "I'm so sorry your majesty. I made so many fairy cakes I couldn't fly, then I just, I just…"

"Now, now," said the Queen. "Come sit down. Here, have a cup of tea and then tell me the whole story."

So Honeywheat told the Queen about the squirrel, then what had happened to Cuddles, and then about the hungry sparrow chicks.

The Queen laughed. "I know those chicks. They almost ate my crown yesterday."

"I'm so sorry I wasn't able to bring you the fairy cakes you wanted for your tea party," said Honeywheat.

The Queen smiled. "I'm the one who must apologize to you. Squirrels are very good at delivering messages quickly, but they do get them muddled up at times."

"What do you mean your majesty?" asked Honeywheat.

"I asked the squirrel to invite you to tea," said the Queen. "When he wasn't sure who you were, I told him 'The one who makes the best fairy cakes in the forest.'" The Queen smiled. "Your fairy-cakes would have been lovely, but I didn't want them. I just wanted your company for tea my dear Honeywheat."

The two fairies laughed and talked for the rest of the afternoon. On her way home, Honeywheat checked in on Cuddles, whose paw was already looking much better. Tired from a long and eventful day, Honeywheat slipped into her flower-petal bed and was soon fast asleep.

The Tri-Planetary Cup

Space racer Annie sat in the Red Racer's captain's chair and clicked her safety harness together. "Come on Max, the race is about to start!"

Max, her robot crew-mate, rolled into his seat next to her. "All locked in Captain. The Red Racer is ready for lift-off."

The viewscreen in front of them blinked to show the Tri-Planetary Cup's race announcer. "Let's start the countdown clock with one minute to go. Get ready everyone!"

"I hope we can figure out the three clues," said Annie as she started the Red Racer's engines.

"We can do it Annie," said Max. "I'm good at remembering things and you're great at figuring out puzzles about planets."

"Thanks Max,' said Annie. "I'll try not to let you down."

The countdown clock began to beep as the Red Racer's engines roared.

"Okay Max, here we go. Three, two, one, lift-off!" shouted Annie as the Red Racer and a dozen other spaceships soared away from the start line and into space.

"First clue coming in Captain," said Max.

The viewscreen blinked to show a picture of a cat playing a fiddle while a cow jumped over a block of cheese.

Max shook his head. "That's a tough one."

"No way, that's easy. It's the moon!" said Annie.

Max blinked his robot eyes. "How does that compute?"

Annie smiled. "In the nursery rhyme the cow jumped over the moon, and some people used to think that the moon was made of cheese. It all fits!"

"Wow," Max said. "Great thinking! I knew you were good at this."

Annie set the Red Racer on course for the Moon while Max used the viewscreen to check on the other racers.

"There are five other racers also heading for the moon," he said.

"That's better than twelve," said Annie.

Max squeaked. "Yes, but one of them is Racer-X!"

Annie's eyes went wide. "He's won this race for the last five years," she whispered. "He'll be tough to beat."

"We can do it Annie," said Max. "You can out-think Racer-X, I know you can."

Annie smiled. "Thanks Max. I'll do my best."

Max reset the viewscreen as they got close to the moon. "Searching for the race beacon. Searching. Found it!"

"Great!" said Annie. "Let's see the next clue."

The viewscreen showed a picture of a hand wearing four rings, each ring a different size. Three of them were silver but the smallest one was gold.

"What does that mean?" Max said as he shook his

head.

"Quick," said Annie. "What planet is known for having rings?"

"How should I know?" moaned Max. "I didn't think any of them had hands!"

Annie laughed. "No silly. Of course planets don't have hands. But Saturn is known for having rings of space dust around it. It must be Saturn!"

The Red Racer changed course for Saturn and soared through space, engines roaring.

Max cheered. "You did it Annie. We're in the lead!"

"Not quite," said Annie. She pointed out of the window at a bright blue spaceship soaring along next to them.

"Racer-X," whispered Max.

Annie nodded. "Yes, and his ship is just as fast as the Red Racer. If we want a chance at winning we'll have to figure out the last clue before he can."

The Red Racer's alarms began to blare. "Watch out Annie!" cried Max. "Asteroids!"

The Red Racer dove and twisted as Annie steered them around the boulders.

"Great flying!" shouted Max as Annie drove the Red Racer out of the asteroid field without a scratch.

Annie wiped the hair back from her face. "Thanks Max, that was close. Is Racer-X okay?"

Max checked the viewscreen. "He is, but he's ahead of us now. How will we ever catch him?"

The two spaceships closed in on Saturn.

"I don't see the race beacon," said Max.

"It must be in one of the rings," said Annie. She looked out of the window. "Racer-X looks confused. Let's get ahead of him." She dove the Red Racer into Saturn's largest dust ring.

"No good," said Max. "There's too much space dust. Are you sure it's here?"

Annie shook her head. "No, it was a guess. I'm sorry Max."

"Don't worry Annie," said Max. "Just think about the clue we were given."

Annie closed her eyes. "There was one ring that was gold. That has to be the ring with the race beacon. What size was it?"

"Thinking. Thinking. Got it!" said Max. "The gold ring was the smallest. The race beacon must be in Saturn's smallest ring."

Annie drove the Red Racer to the smallest of Saturn's rings. "Can you see it now?"

Max began waving his arms. "Yes, and Racer-X is already there!"

"Quick, what's the clue?" asked Annie. The viewscreen showed a picture of a fried egg with a red yolk.

Max groaned. "We're doomed!"

"Calm down Max!" said Annie. "Let's think. On what planet can you find eggs?"

"Earth!" said Max. "Earth is the only place you can find eggs, it must be Earth!"

Just then, Racer-X's spaceship turned and blasted off. Max pointed after it. "He's heading for Earth, Annie. Quick, let's go!"

"Hold on," said Annie. "Eggs are from Earth, but egg yolks are normally yellow, not red."

"What are you thinking?" asked Max.

"The red color is a clue," said Annie. "What planets are red?"

Max beeped and clicked. "Well," he said. "Mars is known as the Red Planet. Do you think it's Mars?"

Annie squinted at the picture of the egg. "No. It's Jupiter. Look. The red yolk looks like a big red spot on the egg. Jupiter is known for having a giant red spot on it. It must be Jupiter!"

Max nodded. "That computes. Let's go!"

Annie set the Red Racer on a course for Jupiter. They watched on the viewscreen as Racer-X's ship returned to Earth.

"We're almost at Jupiter," said Annie.

"And Racer-X is landing on Earth," said Max, peeking at the viewscreen between his fingers. "I almost can't watch!"

The viewscreen blinked to show the race announcer. "Racer-X is out of the race. Earth was not the third planet."

"Quick Max, can you see the race beacon at Jupiter?" asked Annie.

Max looked. His arms began to wave. "I see it Annie. There it is!"

The race announcer on the viewscreen smiled. "Congratulations to Annie and Max of the Red Racer. You've won the Tri-Planetary Cup!"

Annie and Max cheered and hugged. They flew the Red Racer back to Earth where everyone gave them a grand round of applause. Even Racer-X congratulated them on their victory as he handed over the golden trophy of the Tri-Planetary Cup. Annie and Max danced and celebrated until it was very late. When they got into their beds after such an exciting day, it wasn't long before they were both fast asleep and dreaming of flying the Red Racer to victory once again.

The Good Witch

Elsie walked into her grandmother's kitchen and the smell of freshly baked cookies. "Hello grandma. Those smell delicious! May I have one?"

Her grandmother smiled. "Of course my dear. Have a seat while I get some milk for us to drink."

Elsie sat on the kitchen stool as Peter, her grandmother's dog, padded in. "Hey Elsie," Peter said. "Could you give me one of those cookies please?"

Elsie stared at Peter. Peter wagged his tail.

"Whatever's the matter dear?" asked her grandmother as she set two glasses of milk on the table.

"Grandma. Peter asked me for a cookie," said Elsie.

Her grandmother smiled. "You know he likes them dear, go ahead and give him one."

"No grandma, he spoke it. I heard him speak! Real words!" said Elsie.

Elsie's grandmother leaned close to her. "Did you now?"

Peter raised a paw. "Could I have some milk also?"

Elsie pointed at Peter. "Now he wants some milk! Grandma, can you hear him?"

"Yes my dear, all the time." Elsie's grandmother

crunched on a cookie. "If you can hear him also, that means you're like me. A witch."

Elsie nearly fell off her chair. "A witch? How can you be a witch? You're so nice!"

Her grandmother laughed. "Thank you my dear. I do appreciate you saying that. Witches aren't always bad. We use magic, yes, but magic is just another way of getting things done. Since you can hear what animals are really saying, that means you're a witch. But it's what you do with your magic that makes you good or bad." She wiggled her fingers and a cookie floated off the plate to Peter, who happily gobbled it up.

Elsie's eye went wide. "Can you show me how to do that?"

Her grandmother nodded. "I will. First though, every new witch needs to make a magic wand. You need a stick that's the right size and feels right in your hand. You also need a hair from a magic creature."

Elsie looked at Peter. Peter laughed. "Sorry Elsie. It may seem magical to hear me speak, but that's your magic. I don't have any myself."

Elsie's grandmother smiled. "Go check the willow tree for a stick. I'll think about any magical creatures that might live close by."

Elsie went skipping along the pebble-strewn path to the pond on the other side of the hill, where the old willow tree stooped.

"Help me!" someone yelled.

It was a little white goat, stuck in the mud at the pond's edge, under the willow branches.

"Please help me!" yelled the little goat.

Elsie gasped. "Oh dear, of course I will!" She

sprinted down to the pond's edge. The little goat was up to his knees in the mud. Elsie tried to step close enough to pick the goat up, but her own foot got stuck in the mud.

"Careful," said the little goat. "It's really deep and sticky."

"I see that now," said Elsie. She tried to pull her foot out but it was stuck fast. Elsie reached up and grabbed one of the willow branches. "Here," she said as she pulled the branch down so that the end was close to the little goat. "Grab onto that and I will pull you out."

"I'll try," said the little goat. He grabbed the branch with his teeth, but the end broke as soon as Elsie pulled on it.

Elsie took a deep breath. "Okay. I'm coming for you." She leaned out over the mud, holding on to the willow branch to keep from falling in. She put her other arm around the little goat. "Please don't break," she whispered. She pulled on the branch. It creaked but held firm. She pulled even harder. With a POP the little goat came out of the mud! Elsie lost her balance and fell backwards. Her own foot came free with another POP! Then there was a SNAP as the branch broke in her hand.

"Are you okay?" Elsie asked.

"I think so," said the little goat. He tripped on his own feet and fell down. "Maybe I just need to rest for a while."

Elsie stood up, then looked at her muddy foot. Her shoe was lost in the mud. "Let me take you to my grandmother. She will be able to help, I'm sure."

When the little goat nodded she picked him up and

carried him home, wincing every time a pebble on the path jabbed her foot.

"My goodness," said her grandmother when she saw them coming down the hill. "Are you two all right?"

Elsie nodded. "I'm okay grandma, but I think he might be hurt."

The little goat laughed. "I'm okay thanks to you. Please put me down now."

Elsie put the little white goat down. He trotted a few steps away and then in a burst of light transformed into a full grown unicorn! He shook his head and his mane rippled like a rainbow.

"By your selfless act, you have proven you have a good heart," said the unicorn. "I would be honored to give you not one, but three hairs from my mane for your first wand."

Elsie stared at the unicorn. "You know I'm a witch?"

"Yes," said the unicorn. "I know when a new witch is about to get their powers. So I test them to see if they have a good heart, and you most certainly do."

"I just need a stick," said Elsie to her grandmother.

"You have one," said her grandmother.

Elsie looked at her hand. She was still holding onto the branch that broke off from the willow tree. It was just the right size to be a wand and it felt perfect in her hand. She went over to the unicorn, who let her gently pluck three hairs from his mane. "Thank you," Elsie said. "I promise to always do good with my magic."

The unicorn nodded, then charged off and soared into the sky leaving a rainbow in his wake.

Her grandmother sent Elsie for a hot bath, then tucked her into a snuggly bed with a kiss, a plate of cookies and a glass of warm milk.

"You have a rest my dear," said her grandmother. "We'll make your wand tomorrow."

Overcome by all the exciting events of the day, the good witch Elsie soon fell fast asleep.

Manufactured by Amazon.ca
Bolton, ON

18736132R00025